NIKI SMITH
CROSSPLAY

edited by
C. Spike Trotman

book design by
Matt Sheridan

proofread by
Abby Lehrke

quiry@ironcircus.com   www.ironcircus.com

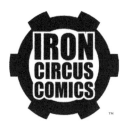

IRON CIRCUS COMICS
™

trange and amazing

For **Kiri**

and the fandoms

that brought us together.

This book would not exist

without the help of

Aleks, **Miles**, **Quinn**,

Kori, and **Sarah**.

Thank you.

first printing: January 2018   printed in Canada   ISBN: 978-1-945820-14

KLIK
KLIK

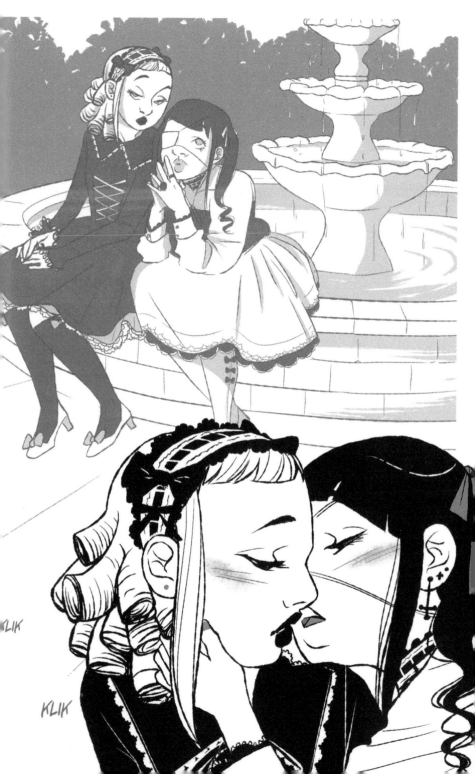

HAHA
KLIK
WOO!
KLIK
KLIK
KISS! KISS!
KLIK
KLIK
KLIK
ONE MORE POSE?
YOU LOOK **SO** GOOD!

EEZ,
RIYA!
FIVE MINUTE BREAK!
HA HA
I'M MELTING IN THIS THING!
SLIP
OH!
HA HA HA
HA
FIRST TIME?

WELCOME TO *MEGACON*.
MEGA

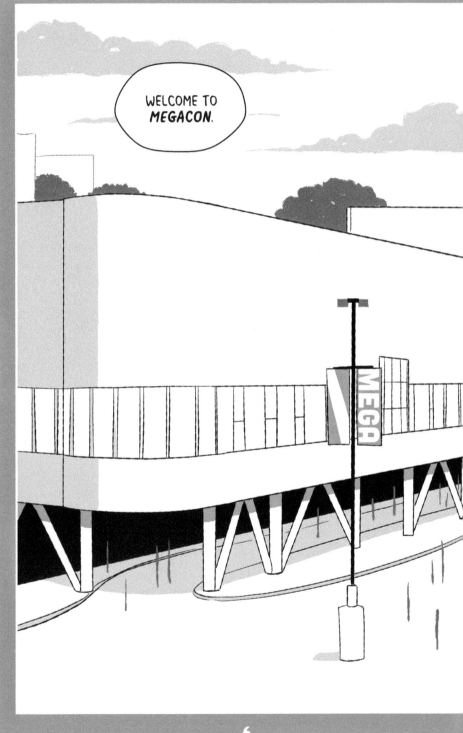

ONE

MEGA
MEGA

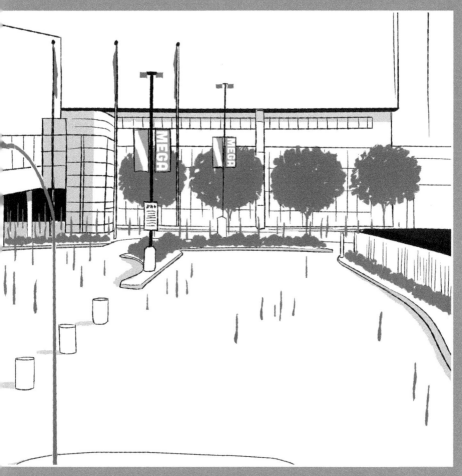

BZZZZZ
WAIT! THE SCAR GOES ON THE OTHER SIDE.
ラーメ
ARE WE MEETING UP IN THE BAR TONIGHT?
I CAAAN'T, MY BIRTHDAY'S NOT 'TIL JULY!
THEY KICKED US OUT LAST YEAR.

SHIT, WHO HAS CONCEALER? I DIDN'T THINK ABOUT MY TATTOO...
OOH, YOU CAN DO THAT? CAN YOU COVER THE ONE ON MY SHOULDER?
ARE YOU SURE YOU DON'T WANNA COSPLAY, JILLIAN? WE GOT YOUR ROW WIG AND EVERYTHING!
I CAN'T... I CAN'T GET THIS DUMB THING WET.
JEEZ, THAT SUCKS.
RIGHT? WE SPENT HOURS ON THE COSTUME...
HEY, THIS 302? I GOT A TEXT...
NOK NOK

LEE! HEY GUYS!
KLAK
HEY! I HEARD A RUMOR ABOUT AN EXTRA BED FOR TWO POOR, ABANDONED COSPLAYERS...?
OUR ROOMIES DECIDED TO DITCH US.
801

HOLD ON, THAT WAS THE HOTEL'S FAULT, NOT MINE! I BOOKED A DOUBLE!
SUURE, SURE. HEY GUYS! I'M LEE.
THEY/THEM PRONOUNS, PLEASE!
SERIOUSLY, SIERRA, YOU GUYS ARE LIFESAVERS.
...I'M MAGGIE!
OF COURSE! WE WOULDN'T LEAVE YOU STRANDED AFTER YOU DROVE ALL THIS WAY.
KATIE!
SHE/HER'S GOOD!
I THINK WE MET AT BENTOCON!
HA HA
BENTO...
OH YEAH, I THINK SO! LAST YEAR, RIGHT?
GOD, WAS *THAT* A SHITTY HOTEL...

AND THIS IS JILLIAN!
...HEY.
HEY.
GOOD TO MEET YOU–
LEE!

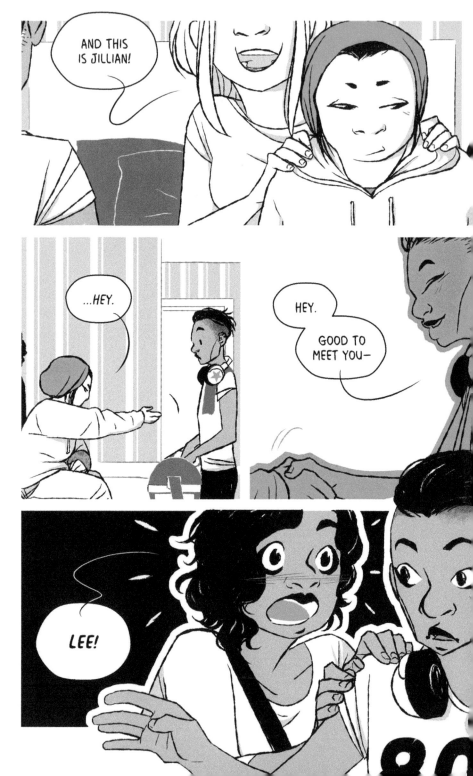

UH, HEY, PRIYA. THANKS FOR THE SPARE BED!
WHO'STHAT WITHYOU??!
I HAVEN'T SEEN THE NEWEST SEASON... **MOTLEY**? **MELODY**?
MEDLEY! FROM THE **WORLD'S END** ARC.
NOT THE CHARACTER!
DO YOU THINK SHE'D— HEY'D?— MODEL FOR ME...?
SHE. DON'T SEE WHY NOT! ALEXIS IS COOL.
SHE'S WITH THE **OVERGROUND** GROUP, I THINK?
SIERRA'S DOING SOMETHING WITH THEM, TOO. WHY? YOU GOT A CRUUUSH?

NO! I JUST THINK SHE'D MAKE A GOOD MODEL!
I KNOW, I KNOW. BUT SHE DOES MAKE A PRETTY HOT GUY, HUH?
YEAH...

WE COULD POSE WITH THE OARS.
KLIK
HERE, THIS BIT—
AW, I MISS THE OLD UNIFORMS!
I KNOW, ME TOO!
LIFT YOUR CHIN...

KLIK

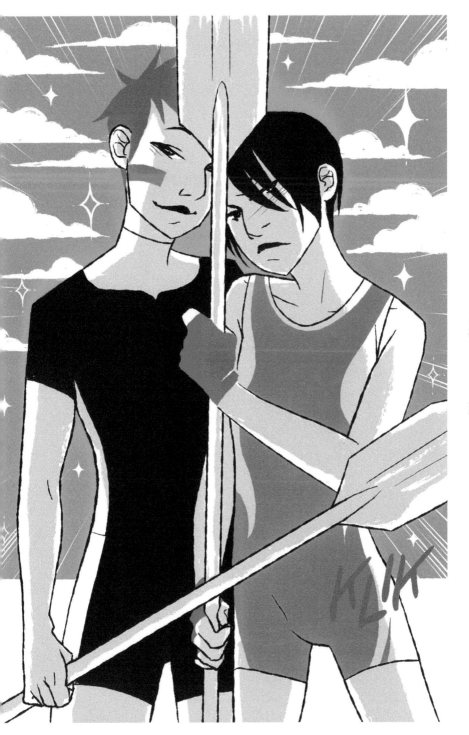

フェイク☆アニメ
ROW!

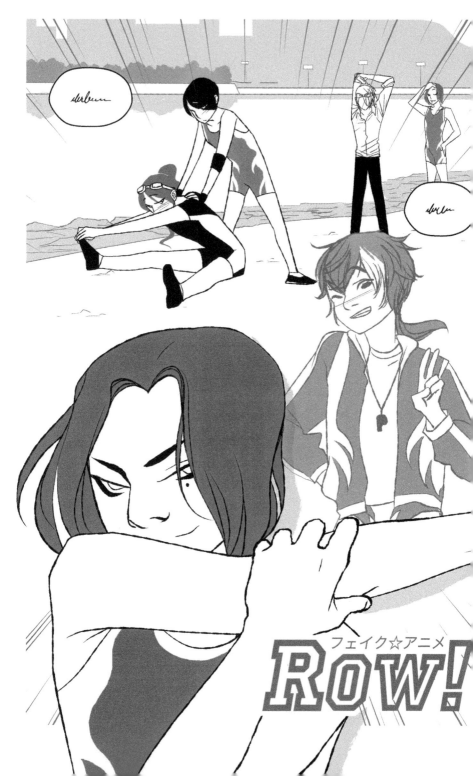

AKITO IS **SO** NOT A TOP.
WHAAT, HE IS! HE SO IS!
JUST 'CUZ HE'S SHORTER DOESN'T MEAN—
HA HA HA
THAT'S NOT WHAT I MEAN!

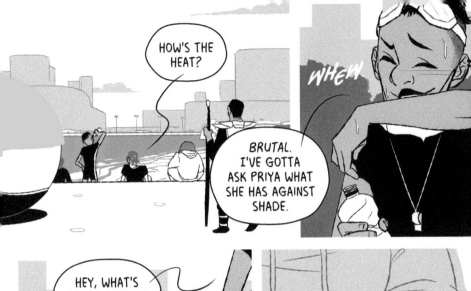

HOW'S THE HEAT?

WHEW

BRUTAL. I'VE GOTTA ASK PRIYA WHAT SHE HAS AGAINST SHADE.

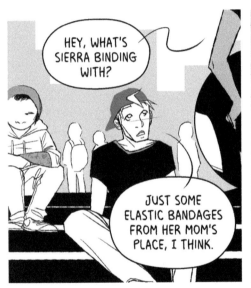

HEY, WHAT'S SIERRA BINDING WITH?

JUST SOME ELASTIC BANDAGES FROM HER MOM'S PLACE, I THINK.

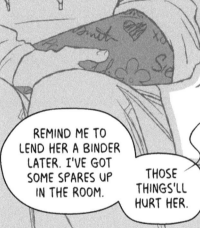

REMIND ME TO LEND HER A BINDER LATER. I'VE GOT SOME SPARES UP IN THE ROOM.

THOSE THINGS'LL HURT HER.

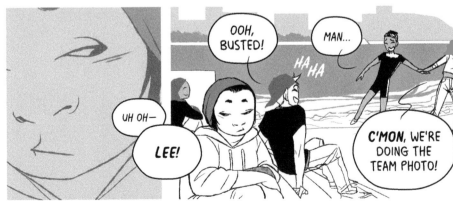

OOH, BUSTED!

MAN...

HA HA

UH OH—

LEE!

C'MON, WE'RE DOING THE TEAM PHOTO!

20

HA HA HA
HURRY, WE'VE GOTTA GET TO A PANEL AFTER!
ANOTHER ONE?!
JEEZ, YOU'R HEAVY
STOP BREAKING CHARACTER!
HA HA HA HA HA

SHFF
TOMMY!
WHAT DO YOU THINK

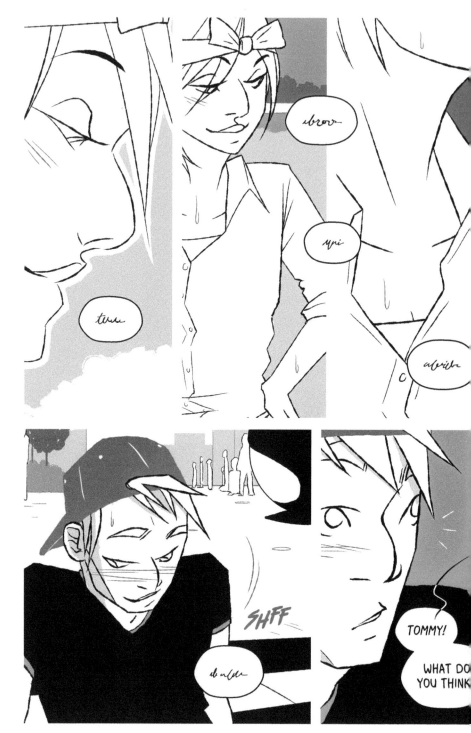

IS YOUR GIRLFRIEND A HOT GUY OR WHAT?
THE **HOTTEST**.
HA HA HA

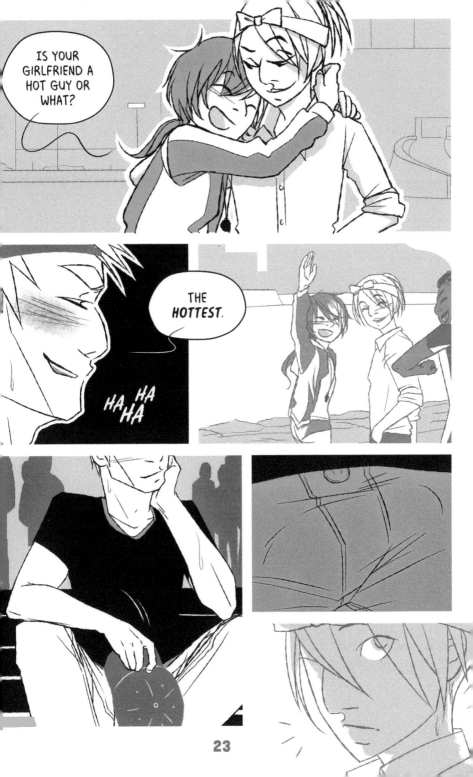

...
SORRY, CREW. I THINK I LEFT MY WALLET BACK UP IN THE ROOM.
I'LL CATCH YOU GUYS IN THE DEALER'S HALL, 'K?
LATER!

TWO

DO NOT
DISTURB
THE HOTTEST, HUH...?

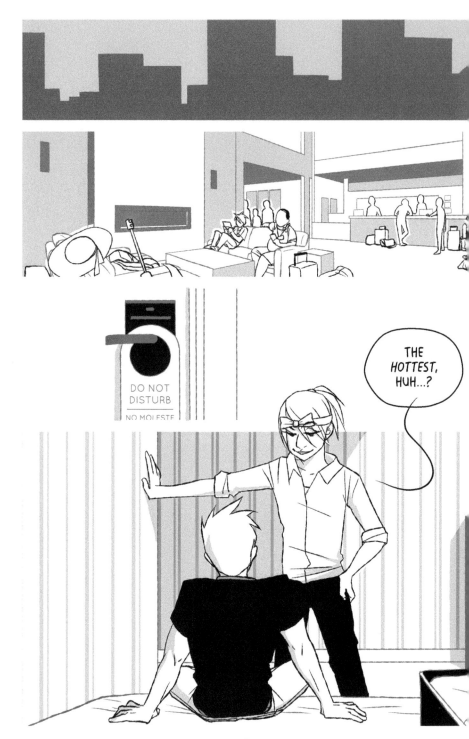

WELL...?
I THOUGHT I SAW YOU SQUIRMING OUT THERE.
WERE YOU THINKING ABOUT ME PACKING, TOMMY? HM?
SHFF

YOU JUST... LOOKED REALLY GOOD.
OH, IS *THAT* ALL.
AND WHAT EXACTLY DID YOU LIKE?
...YOUR HAIR LOOKS GOOD UP.
OH, RIGHT.
HA HA
YOU KNOW HOW MUCH CONCEALER I HAD TO USE TO COVER UP THAT HICKEY YOU GAVE ME?

BRAT.
MM—
AH...
HAA
—!
TOMMY...
...YOU'LL LAUGH...

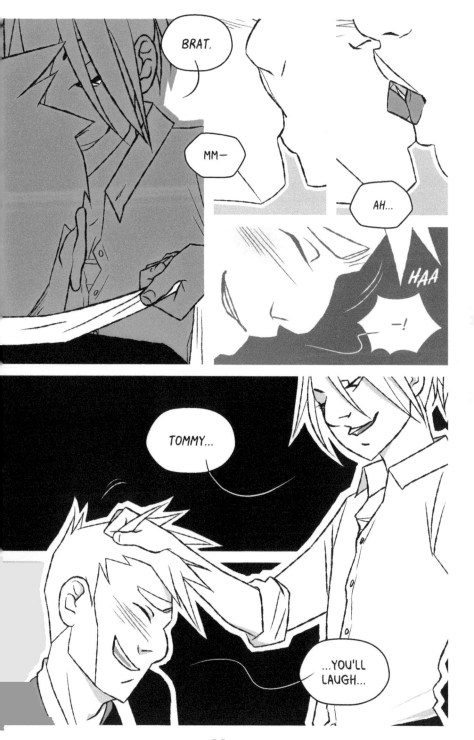

AH...
HM..? LAUGH AT WHAT?
MY— AH... WHEN I...
WHEN I PACKED OUR BAGS...
SHIT— SIERRA— !!
AH...
...OH, SWEETIE.
HAH...
DID YOU THINK I DIDN'T KNOW?

NN...
AH...
SIERRA...

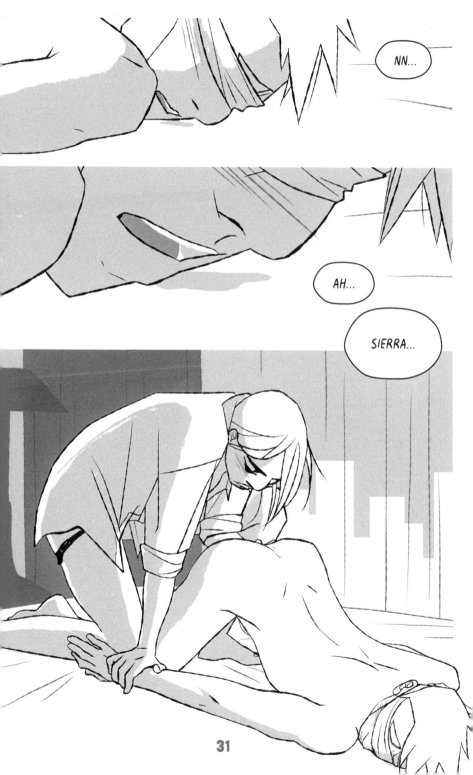

NGH
AH...
NN...
AH...
HAH...
AH...
WHAT? YOU WANT TO TOUCH YOURSELF?
NN—
HMM?
TWITCH

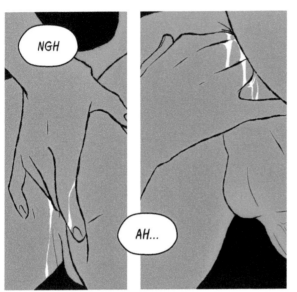

AH...
AH
HAA
NN...
HAA
HAA

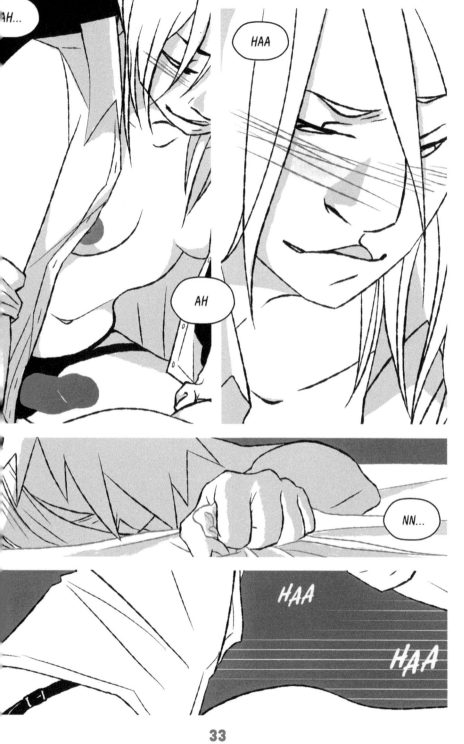

HAA
AH...
HAA
AH
NN...

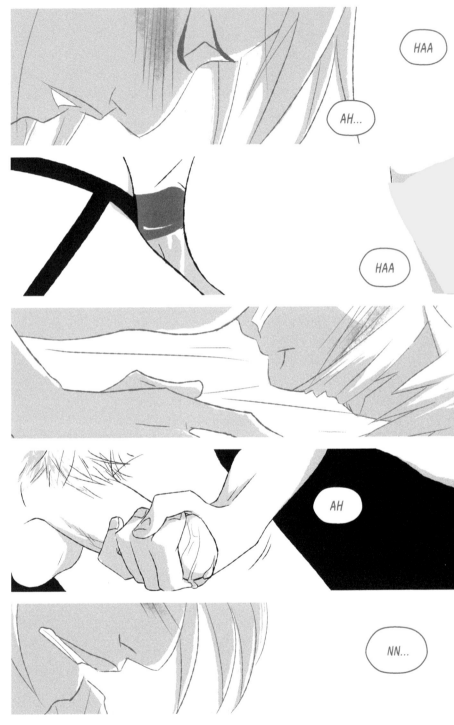

HAH...
HAH...

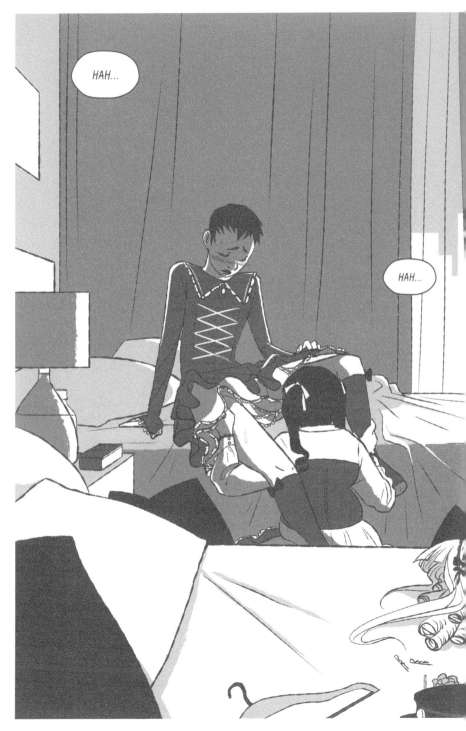

HAH
AH...
HAH...
AH...
AH...
...SOUNDS LIKE SOMEONE *ELSE* IS HAVING FUN.
NGH...

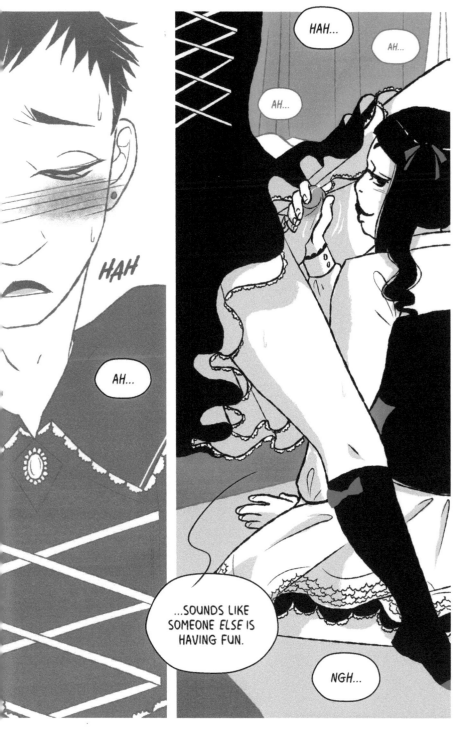

CAREFUL...
AH!
I'M NOT SEWING YOU ANOTHER DRESS IF YOU GET THIS ONE DIRTY.
AH...!

THREE

MEGACON
WEEKEND

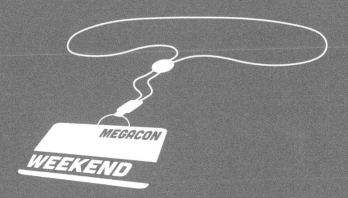

DO NOT DISTURB
NO MOLESTE

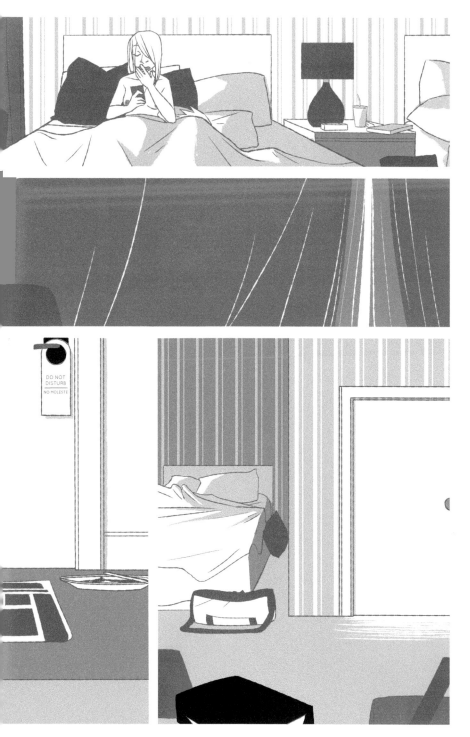

HOW DO THESE THINGS EVEN STAY ON...?
HHN?
WHAT DID YOU SAY? IT'S HARD TO HEAR OVER THE WATER...

!
UH— JUST— THE HORNS, I MEAN—
OH! THERE'S SPECIAL GLUE STUFF YOU CAN GET FOR SKIN.
YOU WOULD NOT BELIEVE HOW MUCH GLUE GOES INTO SOME COSPLAY.
I CAN BARELY SEW AT ALL.
..UH HUH.
...NICE.
UM-
WHY, YOU WANNA TRY 'EM ON?
SQUEAK!
NO!
NOPE. NOT MY THING.
WHAM

AW, C'MON! IT'S FUN! ♥
I'LL STAY ON THE OTHER SIDE OF THE CAMERA, THANK YOU~
...
!
NOK
WHAT ARE YOU TWO **DOING** IN THERE?
NOK
I TOLD YOU, NO MAKE OUTS WHILE THE REST OF US ARE STILL HERE!

JUST A MINUTE, JEEZ! PERVERT!
DON'T MAKE DUMB JOKES!
WHO'S JOKING?
LEE! OUT! ~GIRLS ONLY~!
GIRL, I HAVE SEEN YOUR SCRAWNY BUTT SO MANY TIMES—
YEAH, 'CAUSE YOU'RE PRACTICALLY MY—
OOF!
SIBLING—

—WHO IS NEVERTHELESS AN ENORMOUS BUTTHEAD!
AW, PRIYA, I LOVE YOU TOO.
AND ANYWAY, EMI IS IN HERE TOO, SO BE NICE!
THIS IS TRUE. SORRY, EM'!
HA HA
WE'RE ALMOST DONE, PROMISE!

I SWEAR, IF I MISS THIS PANEL...
WHAT IS IT, ANYWAY?
VOICE ACTING! I KINDA WANNA GIVE IT A TRY...
ISN'T YOUR VOICE STILL CHANGING?
I THINK IT'S ALMOST SETTLED?
MMM. THAT'S WHAT YOU SAID TWO MONTHS AGO.

AW, C'MON... I WON'T SOUND LIKE A TEENAGER FOREVER!
I'M SORRY. WE DIDN'T MEAN TO TEASE. YOU SOUND GREAT.

xoxo

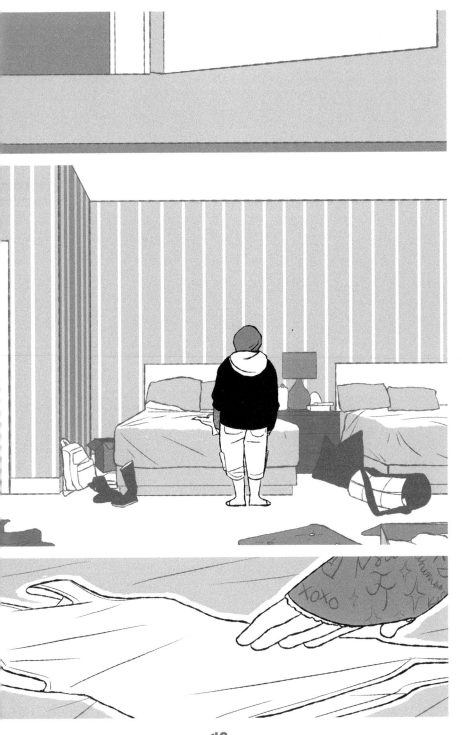

SIGH...
SQUE
STUPID...

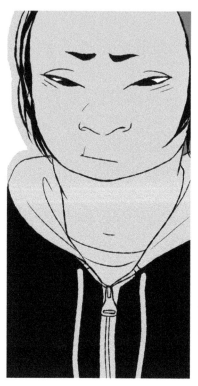

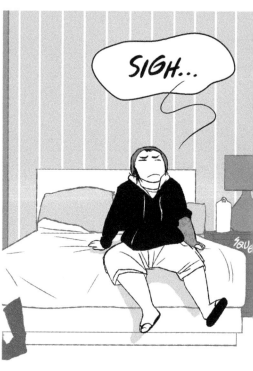

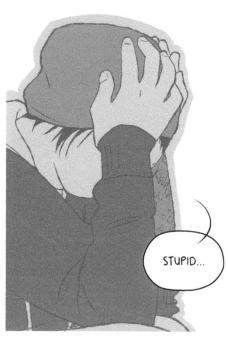

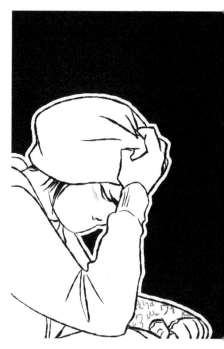

XOXO
Get well Soon

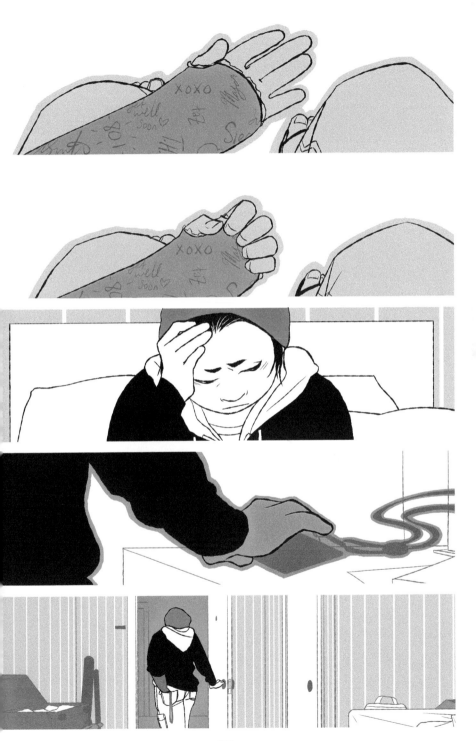

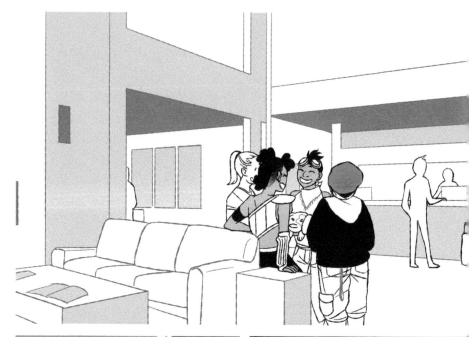

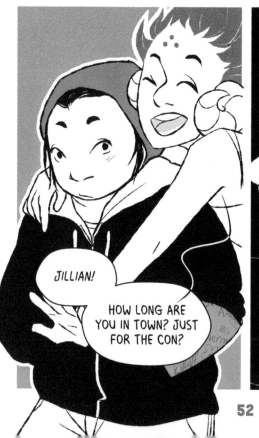

JILLIAN!

HOW LONG ARE YOU IN TOWN? JUST FOR THE CON?

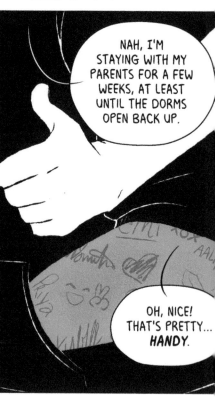

NAH, I'M STAYING WITH MY PARENTS FOR A FEW WEEKS, AT LEAST UNTIL THE DORMS OPEN BACK UP.

OH, NICE! THAT'S PRETTY... *HANDY*.

OKAY, **OFF**.
NO, SERIOUSLY, HOW'S THE ARM?
I HEARD YOU GOT TO SKIP FINALS AND EVERYTHING.
YEAH, THE ONE UP SIDE. IT SUCKS, THOUGH. SERIOUSLY.
GOD, I BET.
AT LEAST YOU GOT TO MAKE IT TO THE CON, THOUGH, RIGHT?
IT'S SO GOOD TO GET THE GANG BACK TOGETHER!
MY SISTER'S HERE THIS YEAR WITH HER BUDDIES. I FEEL LIKE I'M PASSING THE TORCH...
DON'T LET THEM SEE YOU IN THAT GET UP. YOU'LL MORTIFY HER.
ARE YOU ***KIDDING?*** MORTIFYING HER IS WHAT I ***LIVE*** FOR.

HEY, WHO WAS THAT NEW COSPLAYER WITH THE *ROW!* GROUP?
THE ONE WITH THE AWESOME HAIR?
LEE, I THINK? SHE'S COOL.
YEAH! SHE WAS GIVING ME POINTERS ON PACKING YESTERDAY, WHEN WE HAD THE WETSUITS ON.
WITH **SOCKS**! I FELT KINDA SILLY, BUT SHE TOTALLY KNEW WHAT SHE WAS DOING! SHE—
THEY.
!

AH...
SHIT.
NO, I DID IT TOO... DAMN.
...I FORGOT MY BADGE IN THE ROOM.
I'LL SEE YOU DOWN THERE.

FOUR

I ♥

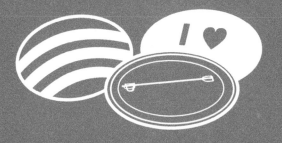

MEGA CON

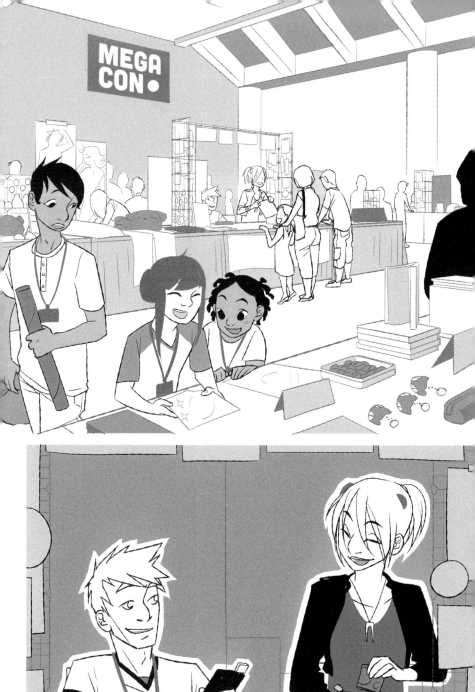

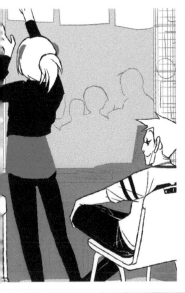

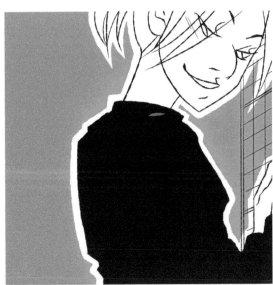

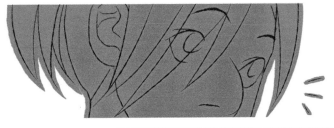

SIERRA!

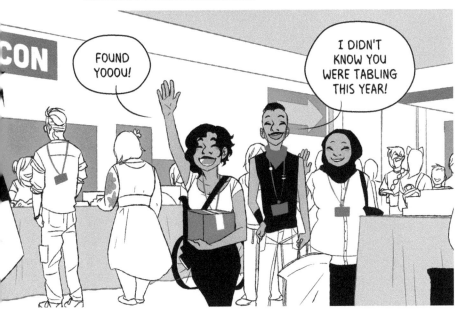

CON

FOUND YOOOU!

I DIDN'T KNOW YOU WERE TABLING THIS YEAR!

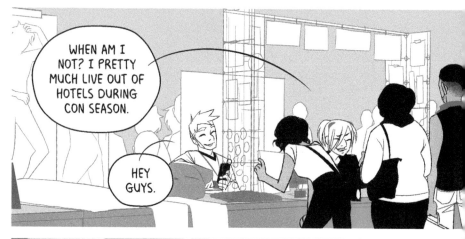

WHEN AM I NOT? I PRETTY MUCH LIVE OUT OF HOTELS DURING CON SEASON.

HEY GUYS.

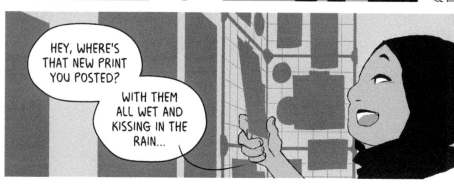

HEY, WHERE'S THAT NEW PRINT YOU POSTED?

WITH THEM ALL WET AND KISSING IN THE RAIN...

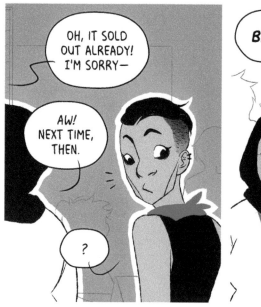

OH, IT SOLD OUT ALREADY! I'M SORRY—

AW! NEXT TIME, THEN.

?

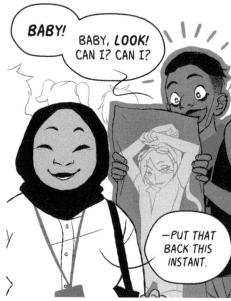

BABY!

BABY, *LOOK!* CAN I? CAN I?

—PUT THAT BACK THIS INSTANT.

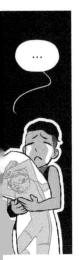

...

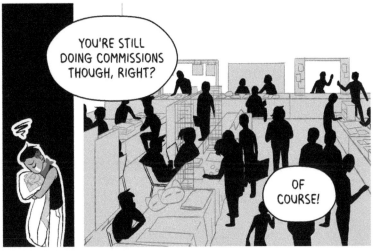

YOU'RE STILL DOING COMMISSIONS THOUGH, RIGHT?

OF COURSE!

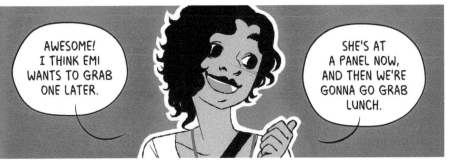

AWESOME! I THINK EMI WANTS TO GRAB ONE LATER.

SHE'S AT A PANEL NOW, AND THEN WE'RE GONNA GO GRAB LUNCH.

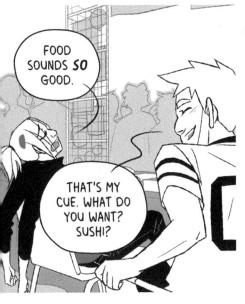

FOOD SOUNDS *SO* GOOD.

THAT'S MY CUE. WHAT DO YOU WANT? SUSHI?

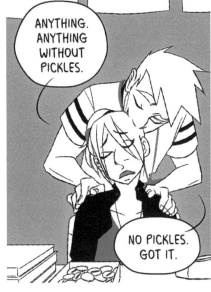

ANYTHING. ANYTHING WITHOUT PICKLES.

NO PICKLES. GOT IT.

07
YOU TWO ARE SO GROSS.
HAHAHA
DON'T I KNOW IT.
WHERE DID YOU TWO DISAPPEAR TO YESTERDAY, ANYWAY?
OH, YOU KNOW. HAD TO FINISH TABLE SET UP.
WELL...
WE WANTED TO GIVE YOU THESE!
OH MY GOD!

WE FIGURE YOU'RE HAVING SOME KIND OF OFFICIAL ENGAGEMENT PARTY...
YOU GUUUUYS!
...BUT SERIOUSLY, CAN WE JUST HAVE A NIGHT WHERE WE GET TO HANG OUT LIKE OLD TIMES AND STREAM FANSUBS UNTIL 4AM?
PLEEEASE?
ONLY IF THERE'S KARAOKE TOO!
OOH! OOH! I CAN DO THE BASS PARTS NOW!
SERIOUSLY?!
WELL... ALMOST~

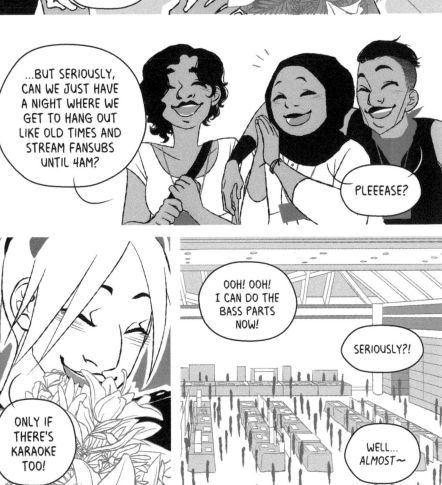

WE'LL CATCH YOU LATER! WE'RE STILL ON FOR DRINKS TONIGHT, RIGHT?
I'LL BE THERE! ARTIST'S ALLEY CLOSES AT 9:00!
C1
BYEEE!
HA HA

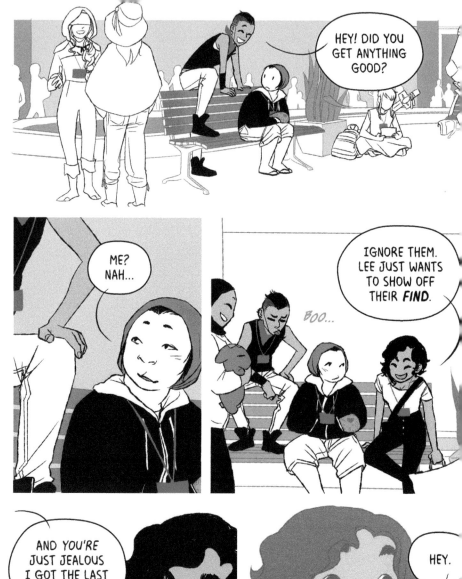

HEY! DID YOU GET ANYTHING GOOD?

ME? NAH...

IGNORE THEM. LEE JUST WANTS TO SHOW OFF THEIR *FIND*.

BOO...

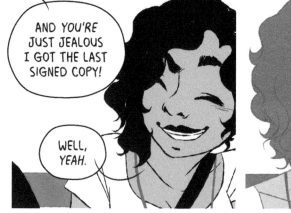

AND *YOU'RE* JUST JEALOUS I GOT THE LAST SIGNED COPY!

WELL, YEAH.

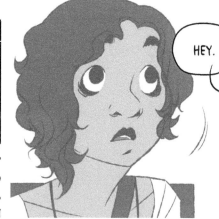

HEY.

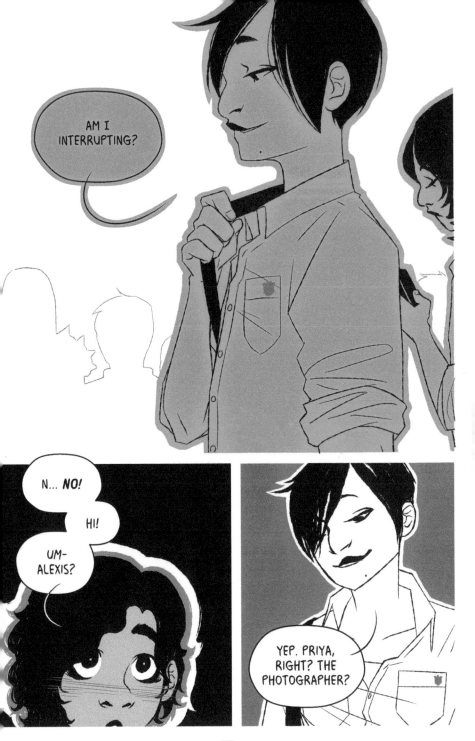

AM I INTERRUPTING?

N... **NO!**

HI!

UM— ALEXIS?

YEP. PRIYA, RIGHT? THE PHOTOGRAPHER?

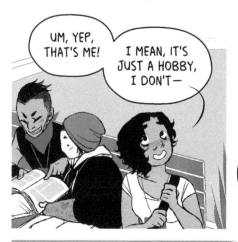

UM, YEP, THAT'S ME!

I MEAN, IT'S JUST A HOBBY, I DON'T—

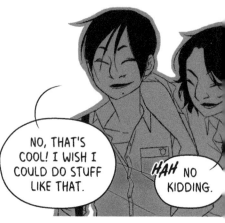

NO, THAT'S COOL! I WISH I COULD DO STUFF LIKE THAT.

HAH NO KIDDING.

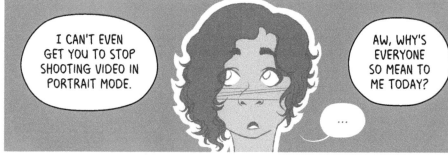

I CAN'T EVEN GET YOU TO STOP SHOOTING VIDEO IN PORTRAIT MODE.

AW, WHY'S EVERYONE SO MEAN TO ME TODAY?

...

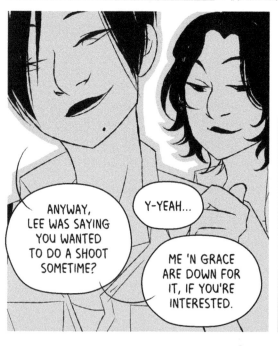

ANYWAY, LEE WAS SAYING YOU WANTED TO DO A SHOOT SOMETIME?

Y-YEAH...

ME 'N GRACE ARE DOWN FOR IT, IF YOU'RE INTERESTED.

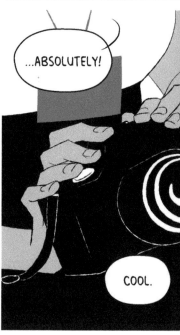

...ABSOLUTELY!

COOL.

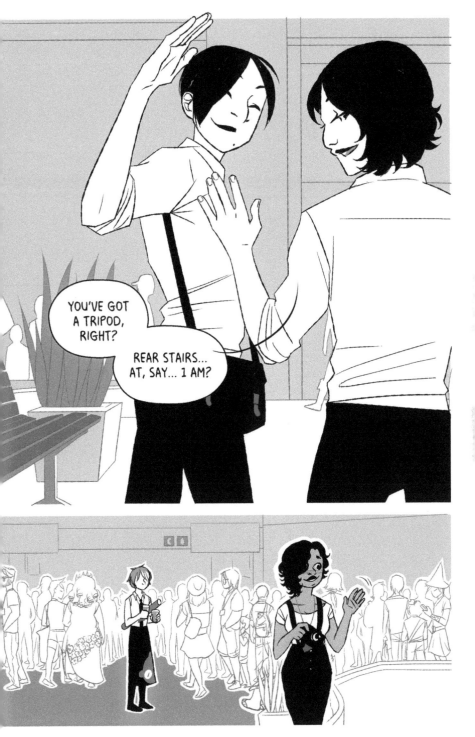

YOU'VE GOT A TRIPOD, RIGHT?

REAR STAIRS... AT, SAY... 1 AM?

...SUP?

EMI!

OH MY GOD!

IS THIS IT? DID YOU GET IT SIGNED? HOW WAS THE PANEL?

HA HA

SO GOOD. HE IS *SO* HOT IN PERSON.

GOD, I BET...

AND SOMEONE ASKED THEM ABOUT FANFIC DURING THE Q&A, AND THEY *KNOW* WHAT *SLASH* IS!

NOO! YOU'RE KIDDING, RIGHT? NO! OH GOD!

TOTALLY SERIOUS.

I BET THE VIDEO'S ALREADY ONLINE.

EMIIII.
WELCOME BACK!
HOW DO YOU DO THIS ALL DAY?
I TOLD YOU TO CHANGE BEFORE THE PANEL!
NEVER WEAR HEELS WHEN YOU KNOW IT'LL BE STANDING ROOM ONLY.
YEAH, BUT WHAT ABOUT MY CHEST? THIS BINDER THING IS *KILLING* ME.
...
!
UGH, THANK GOD THE CON'S ONLY THREE DAYS...
I DON'T KNOW HOW PEOPLE DO THIS, LIKE, EVERY DAY...
WHA—
JILLIAN?

SHE OKAY? WHAT'S UP?
BET HER ARM HURTS.
NO KIDDING. SHE BROKE IT IN THREE PLACES, YOU KNOW? I SAW THE PICTURE.
NOO, STOP TALKING! STOP!
HA HA
...I'M GONNA GO GRAB SOME WATER.
HIBIT HALL C
MEGA

FIVE

I DON'T KNOW WHAT I'M **DOING**.
I DON'T KNOW HOW ANY OF THIS EVEN WORKS.

...CAN YOU BEND YOUR ARM?
CAN I HELP?

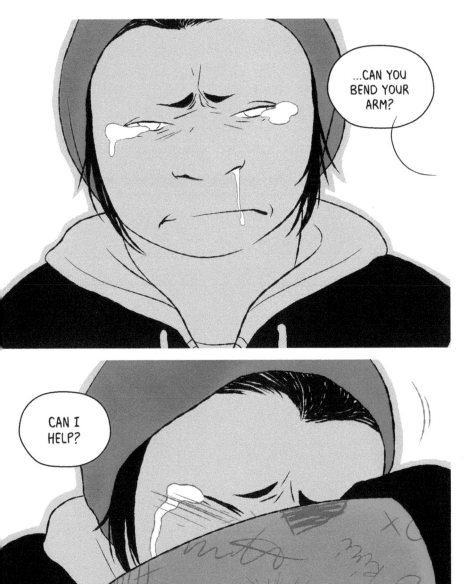

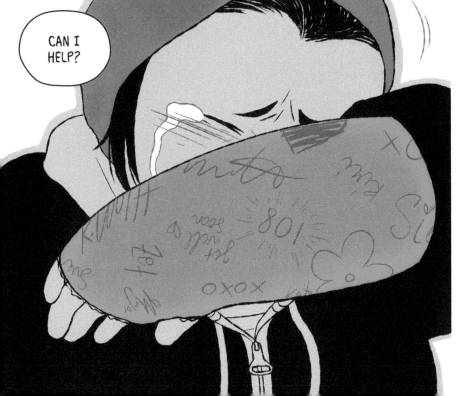

THIS YOUR STUFF? CAN I?
LET'S SEE...
YEAH, THIS IS GOOD. WE CAN WORK WITH THIS.
OH, SHIT, HIDDEN POCKY STASH. NICE.
CHRIST, I HATE BUYING PANTS.
I HAVE TO SHOP IN THE DAMN KIDS' SECTION SOMETIMES...

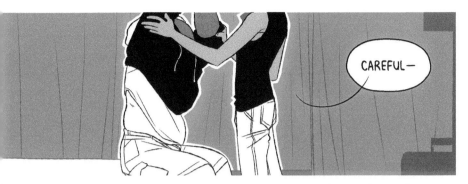

CAREFUL—

IF YOU GIVE YOURSELF A BLOODY NOSE WITH THAT THING, I'M GOING TO CALL YOU A PERVERT. DON'T THINK I WON'T.

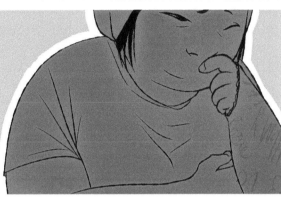

THOSE CASTS SUCK, THOUGH, DON'T THEY?

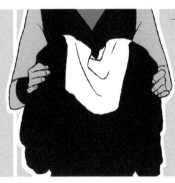

—GO AHEAD AND TAKE THE REST OFF TOO.

CASTS, YEAH. SO DAMN ITCHY, AND **GOD**, DO THEY STINK.
HM, PRETTY SURE THIS ONE IS YOUR SIZE. I KNOW WHERE TO FIND AN EXTRA IF IT ISN'T.
ALL RIGHT, ARMS UP!
I BUSTED MY WRIST WHEN I WAS TEN, TRYING TO IMPRESS MY BROTHERS.
NOT MY BRIGHTEST MOMENT.
ALSO, NOT THE ONLY TIME I'VE FALLEN OFF A ROOF.
OKAY, SO, IF YOU DO THIS ON YOUR OWN, *DON'T FREAK OUT*.
EVERYBODY GETS STUCK THEIR FIRST TIME. YOU'LL GET THE HANG OF IT.

HEY THERE.
SOMEONE'S HARD JUST LOOKING AT HIMSELF.
IS IT THAT OBVIOUS?
...
HA HA HA
SHIT.
YEAH.
IT IS THAT OBVIOUS.

CHUCKLE
YOU KNOW, I CAN GIVE YOU A HAND WITH THAT TOO.
!
...
A BINDER ISN'T THE ONLY THING IN MY BAG OF TRICKS.
WE CAN HAVE WAY MORE FUN THAN THAT.
SH...
SHOW ME.

SHF
SLIP
HAH

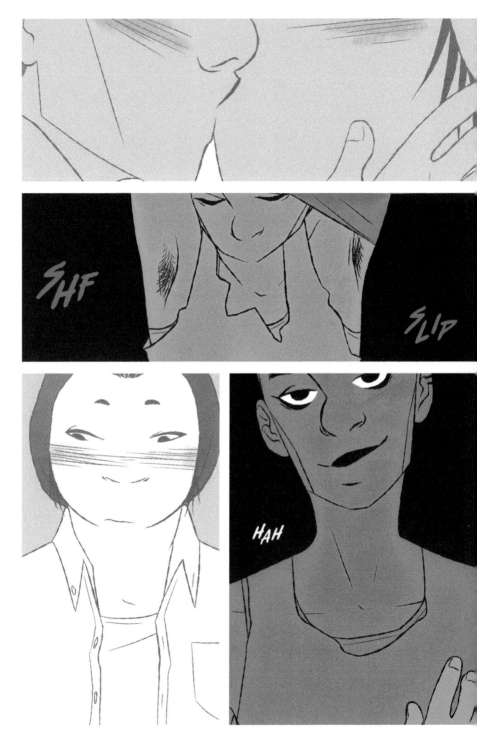

LEE...

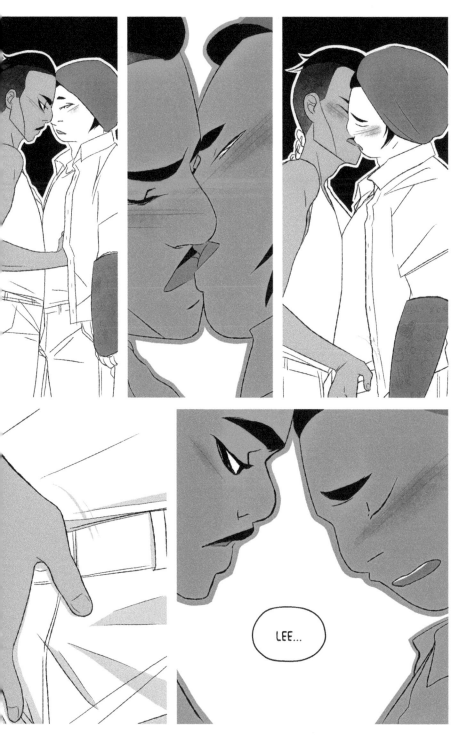

SLIDE
AH...

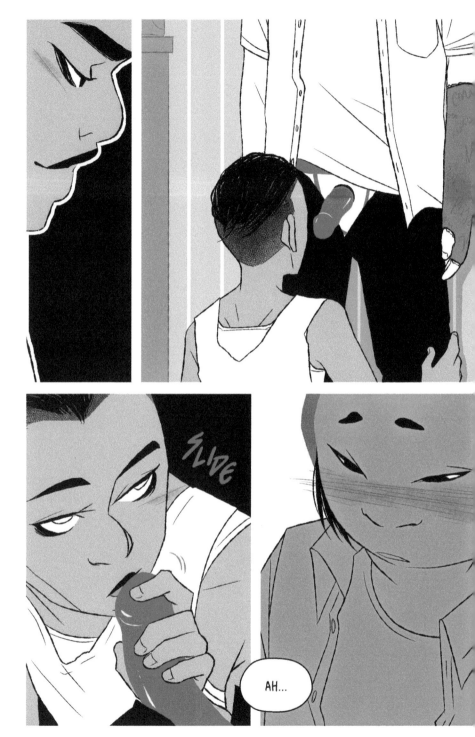

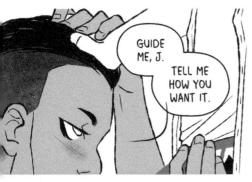

GUIDE ME, J.

TELL ME HOW YOU WANT IT.

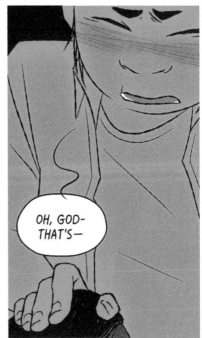

OH, GOD— THAT'S—

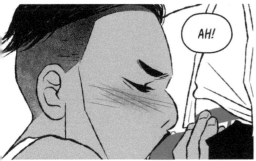

AH!

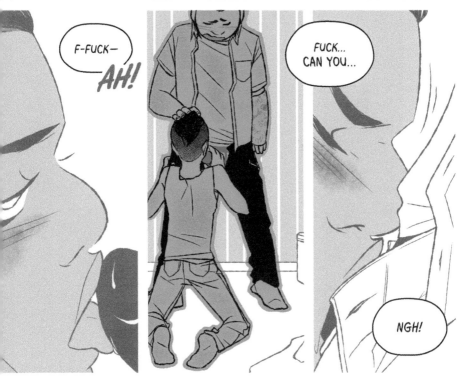

F-FUCK—

AH!

FUCK... CAN YOU...

NGH!

HAA
AH...
HAA
...?
...
MM...

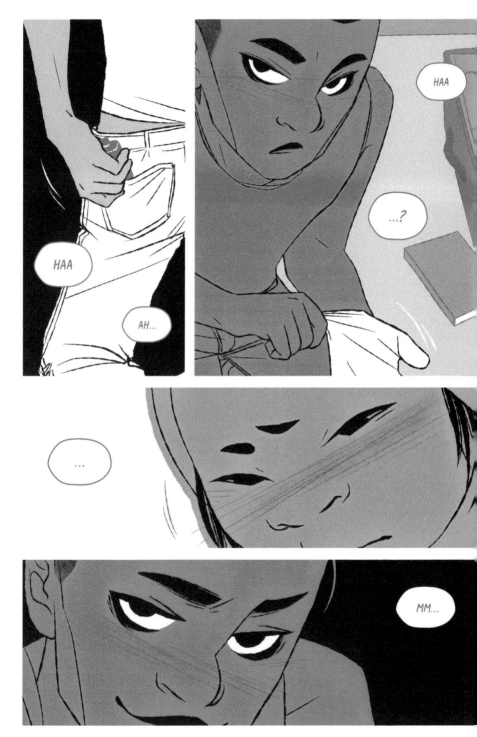

HAH
NN...
AH

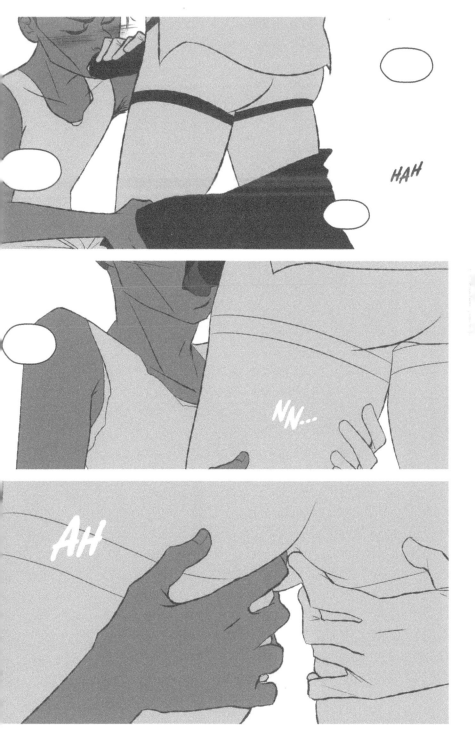

NN...
HAH...
NGH...

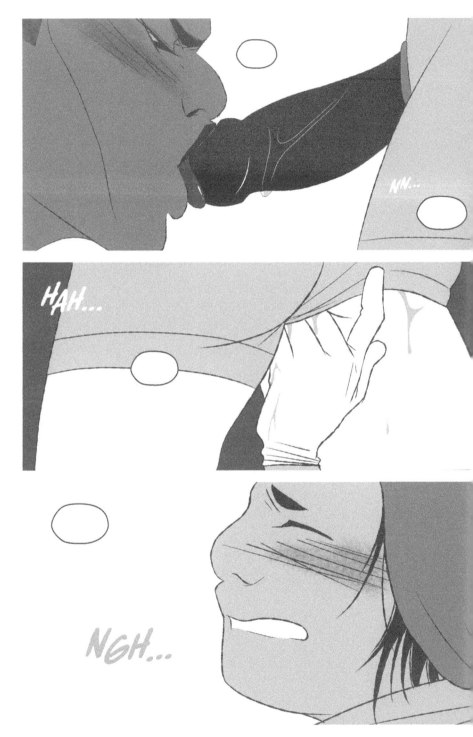

SHLUG
SHLUG
SHLUG

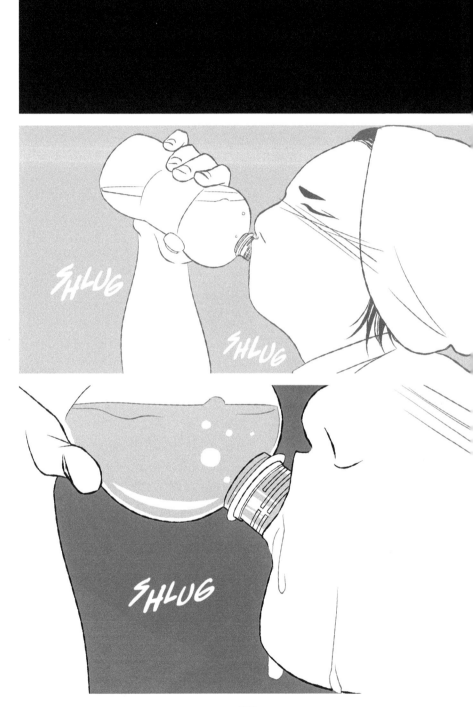

HAA...

HEY. J.
YOU GOOD?
BREATHING
OKAY?

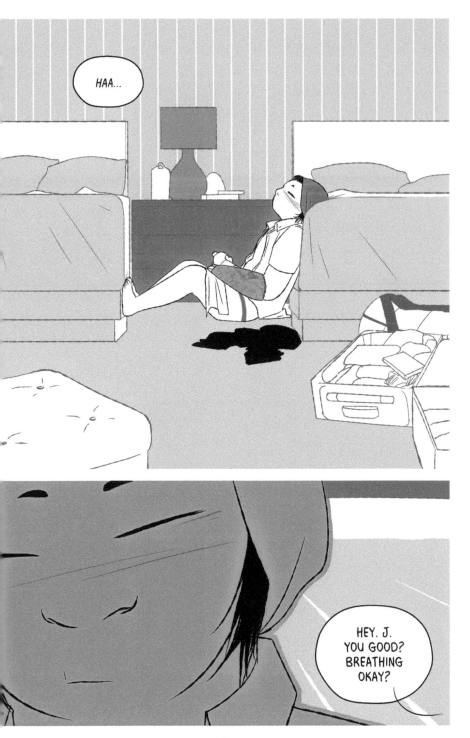

HNN?
OH... YEAH.
I'M FINE.
I MEAN...
IT'S...
IT'S WORTH IT. I KNOW. BUT C'MON, WE GOTTA GET YOU OUTTA THAT.
WHAT—
HEY. SHH. S'OKAY. THE BINDER IS YOURS.
BUT IF YOU'RE GONNA SLEEP, YOU'RE GONNA HAVE TO TAKE IT OFF. COOL?
AH...
YEAH...

...
KLAK
HEY!

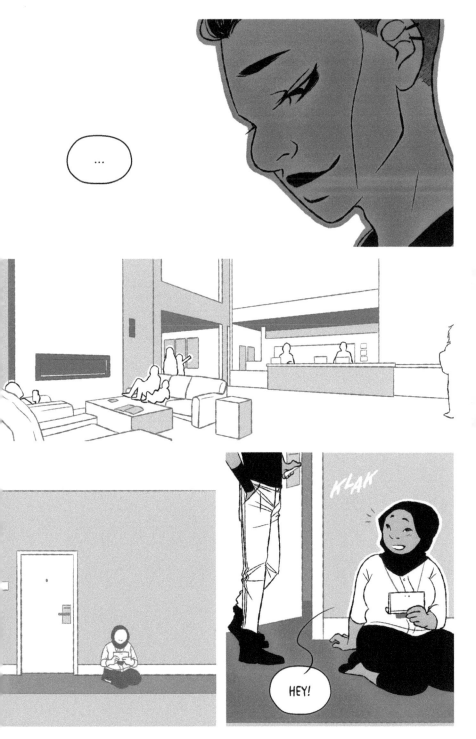

I WAS WORRIED. IS JIL—
J'S GOOD.
IT'S ALL GOOD.
GOOD.

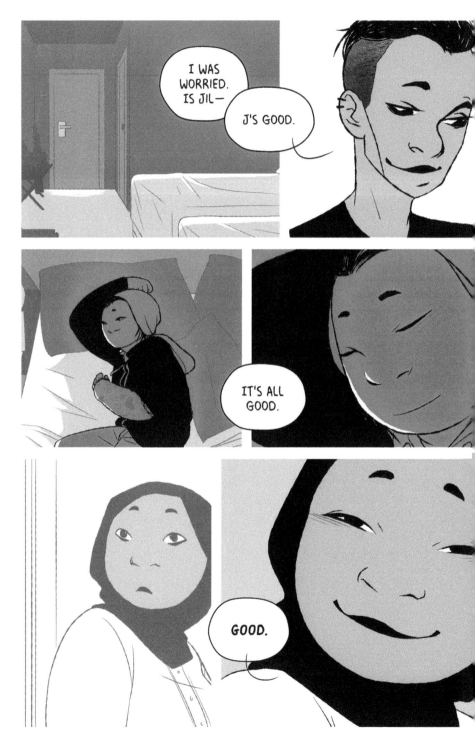

!
LEE!
HN?
HA
HA
HA
HA
WAIT—
YOU DIDN'T GET OFF, DID YOU!

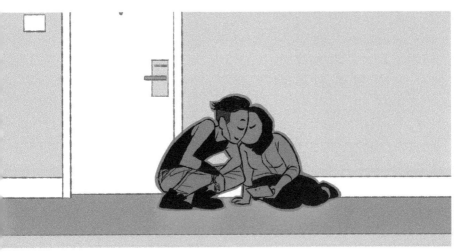

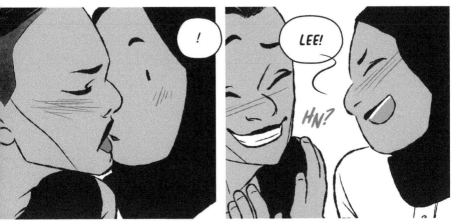

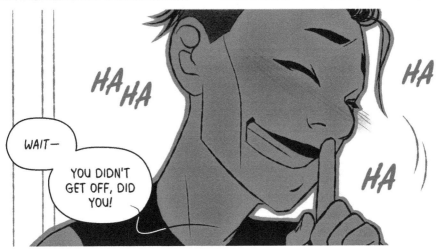

SIX

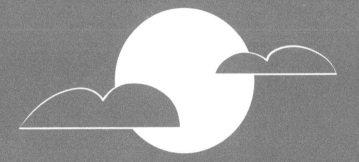

NO ROOF ACCESS
GULP

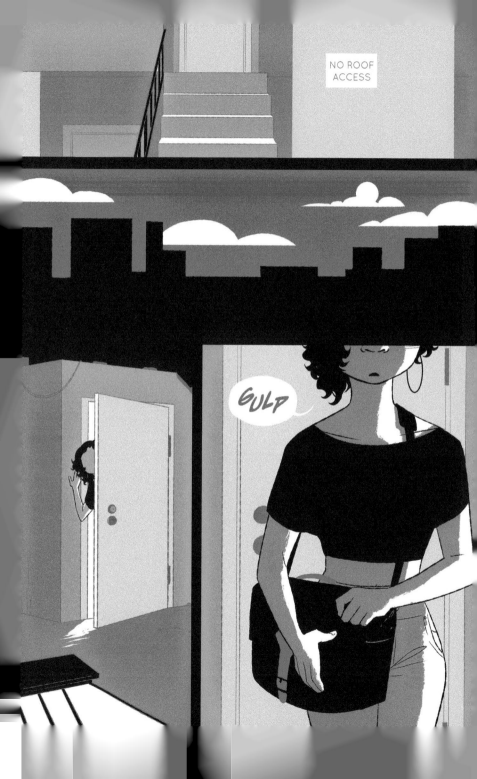

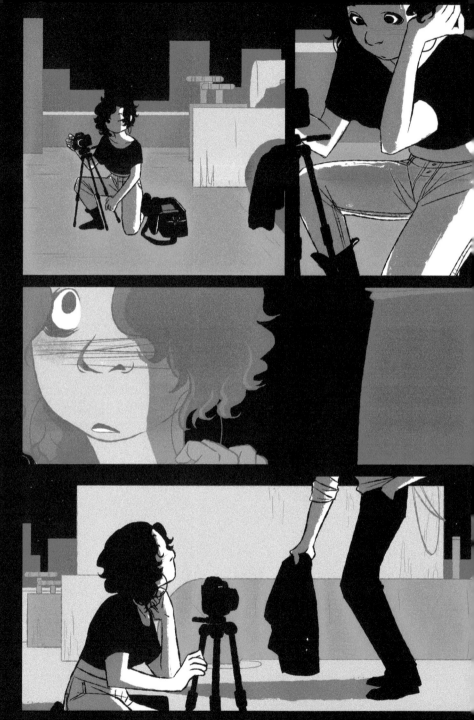

KLIK

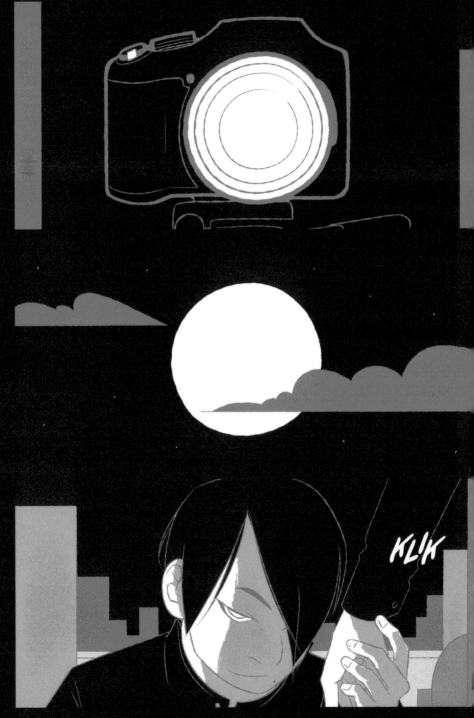

KLIK
KLIK
KLIK
KLIK

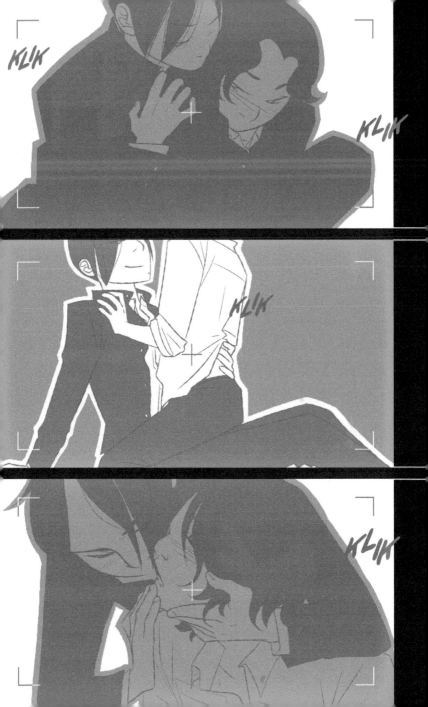

KLIK
KLIK

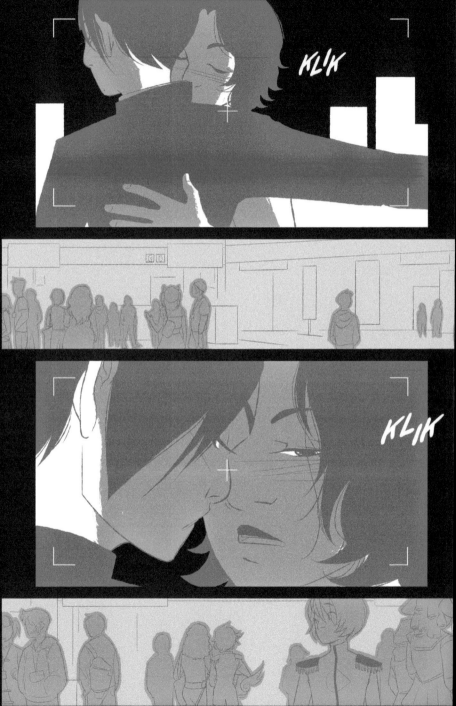

KLIK
KLIK

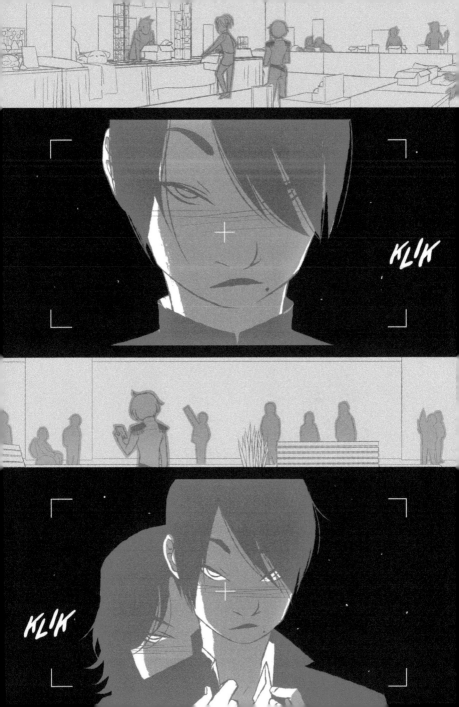

KLIK

CLATTER

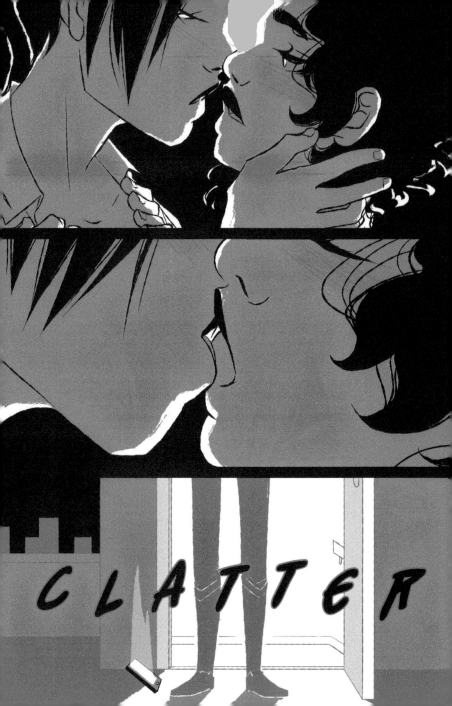

!
–!
?
S–
SORRY...
EMI!

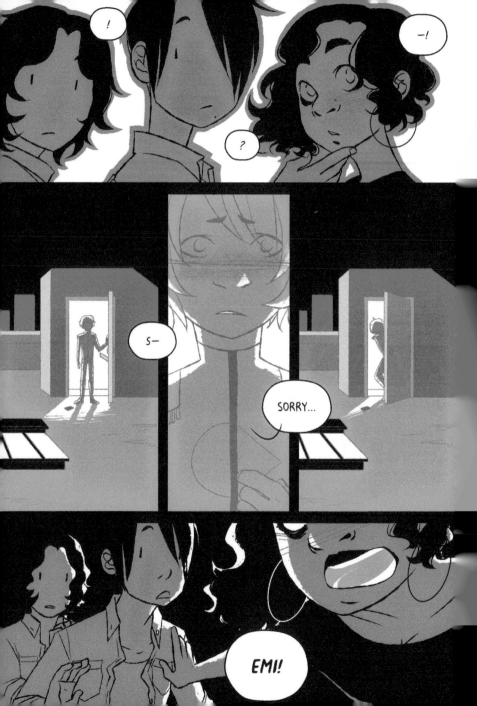

EMI!

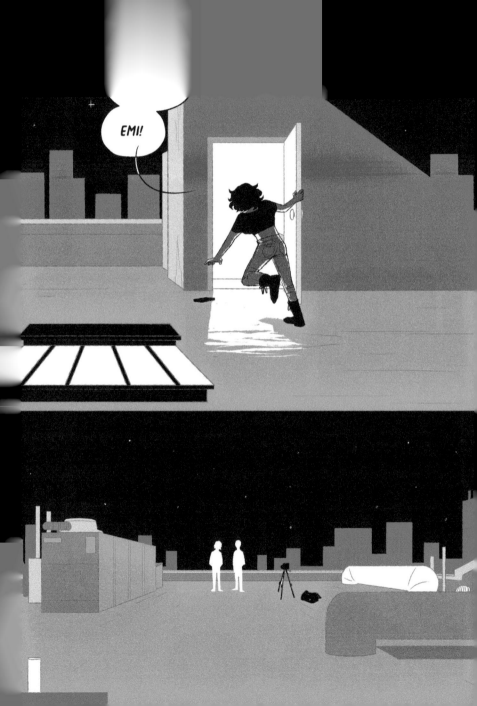

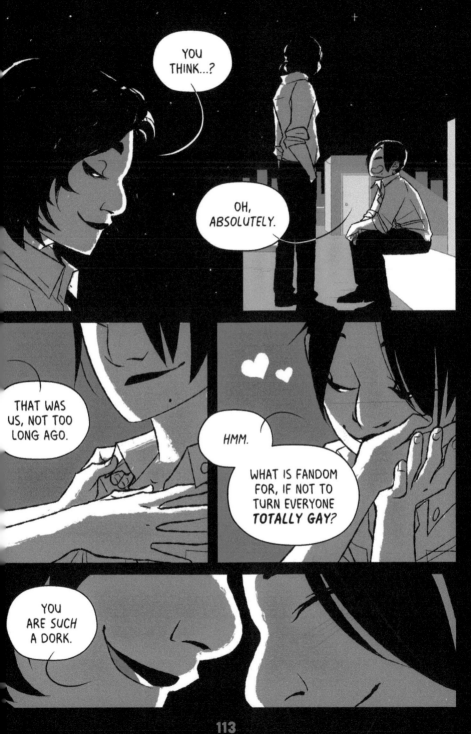

YOU THINK...?

OH, ABSOLUTELY.

THAT WAS US, NOT TOO LONG AGO.

HMM.

WHAT IS FANDOM FOR, IF NOT TO TURN EVERYONE **TOTALLY GAY?**

YOU ARE SUCH A DORK.

SEVEN

HAA
HAA
HAH...

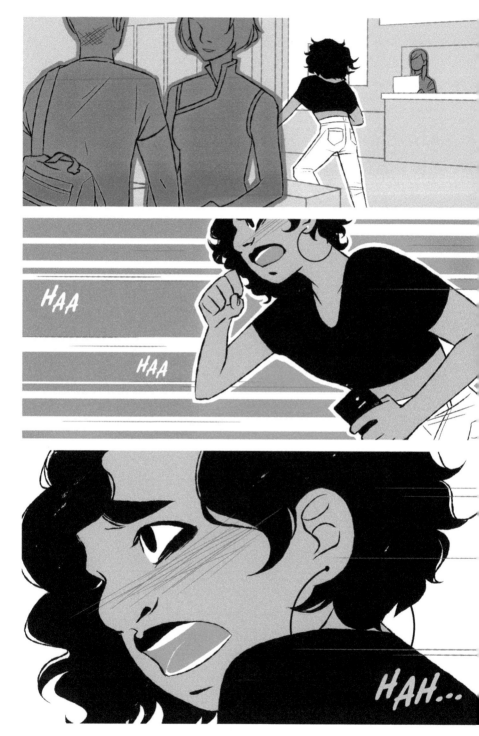

AH—
CLATTER
EMI...? EMI!
RATTLE RATTLE
GO AWAY.
EMI, I'M SOR—
WHY ARE YOU APOLOGIZING!
YOU'RE ALLOWED TO HIC KISS WHOEVER YOU WANT!
I DON'T...
SHE'S JUST—
I DIDN'T THINK YOU EVEN LIKED GIRLS...
I... HIC I WOULD'VE...

SHE'S NOT... WHO I **WANT** TO KISS...
EMI...
I DON'T KNOW WHAT TO DO...
I...
THIS IS ALL... NEW... AND I DIDN'T...
I DIDN'T KNOW IF YOU...

I LIKE YOU.
I LIKE YOU SO MUCH.
I DON'T KNOW HOW TO DO ANY OF THIS!
I HAD LIKE, ONE FAKE BOYFRIEND IN HIGHSCHOOL, AND THIS IS ALL SO NEW TO ME,
AND I DIDN'T THINK I HAD A CHANCE, AND I'M SO TERRIBLE AT THIS.

YOU'RE MY BEST FRIEND
AND I LIKE YOU
AND I DIDN'T WANT TO RUIN ANYTHING
AND NOW I'VE RUINED—

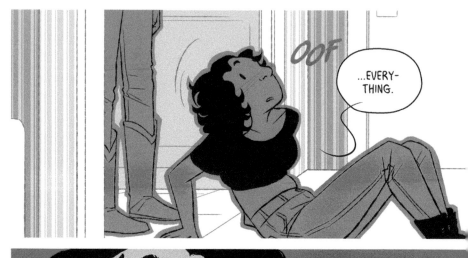

...EVERY-THING.

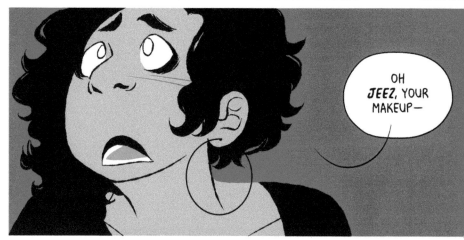

OH *JEEZ*, YOUR MAKEUP—

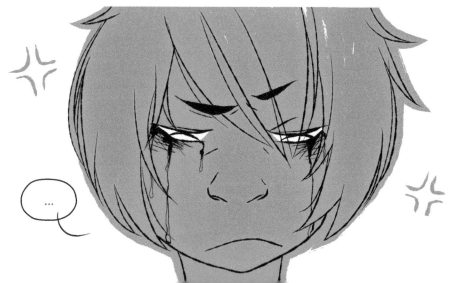

...

NO! I JUST— I'M SORRY I RUINED IT! YOU SPENT AGES ON IT, I SAW YOU—
I MEAN— I'M SORRY—
YOU STILL...
AH—
YOU'RE STILL... UNBELIEVABLY CUTE.
...
...YOU MEAN IT?
EMI...
CAN I... CAN I KISS YOU? EMI?

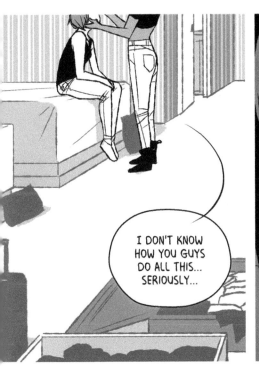

I DON'T KNOW HOW YOU GUYS DO ALL THIS... SERIOUSLY...

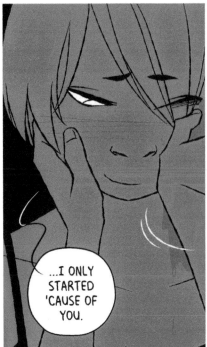

...I ONLY STARTED 'CAUSE OF YOU.

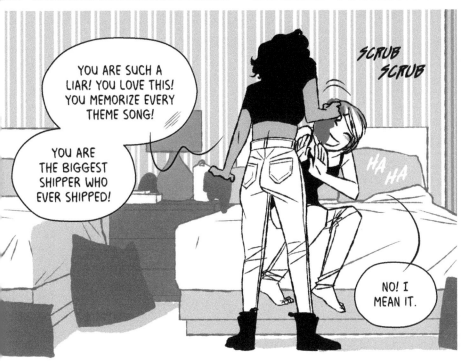

YOU ARE SUCH A LIAR! YOU LOVE THIS! YOU MEMORIZE EVERY THEME SONG!

YOU ARE THE BIGGEST SHIPPER WHO EVER SHIPPED!

SCRUB SCRUB

HA HA

NO! I MEAN IT.

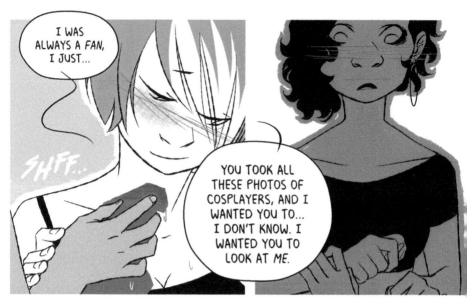

I WAS ALWAYS A *FAN*, I JUST...

SHFF...

YOU TOOK ALL THESE PHOTOS OF COSPLAYERS, AND I WANTED YOU TO... I DON'T KNOW. I WANTED YOU TO LOOK AT *ME*.

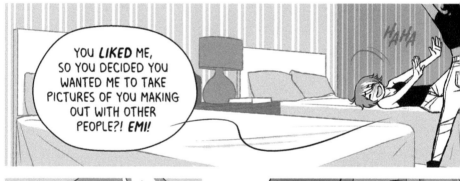

YOU *LIKED* ME, SO YOU DECIDED YOU WANTED ME TO TAKE PICTURES OF YOU MAKING OUT WITH OTHER PEOPLE?! *EMI!*

HAHA

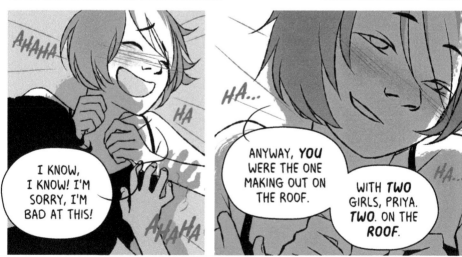

AHAHA

HA...

HA

AHAHA

I KNOW, I KNOW! I'M SORRY, I'M BAD AT THIS!

ANYWAY, *YOU* WERE THE ONE MAKING OUT ON THE ROOF.

WITH *TWO* GIRLS, PRIYA. *TWO*. ON THE *ROOF*.

HA...

YEAH. UM. THAT WAS A FIRST FOR ME TOO.
!
IT'S OKAY. I TOTALLY WOULD'VE TOO. ♥
EMI!
GASP
NOT ALLOWED. ONLY ME. ONLY KISS ME.
HMPH
I MEAN... IF THAT'S OKAY WITH YOU.
...I'D LIKE THAT.
SHF

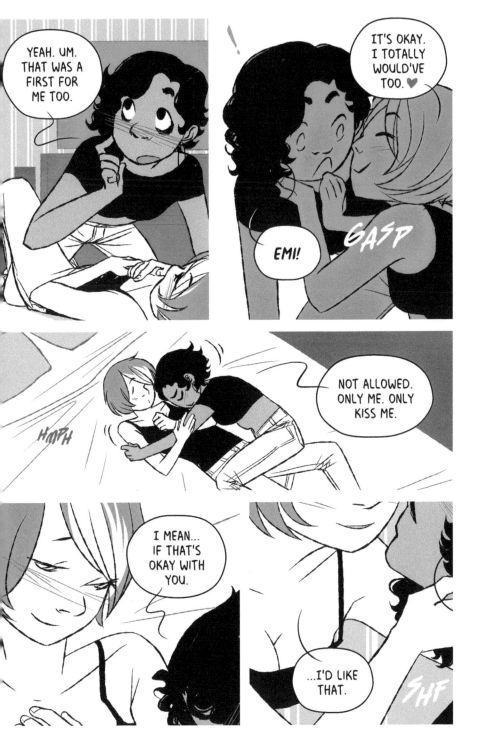

I'D...
I'D LIKE... MORE THAN THAT.
FWIP!
HA HA

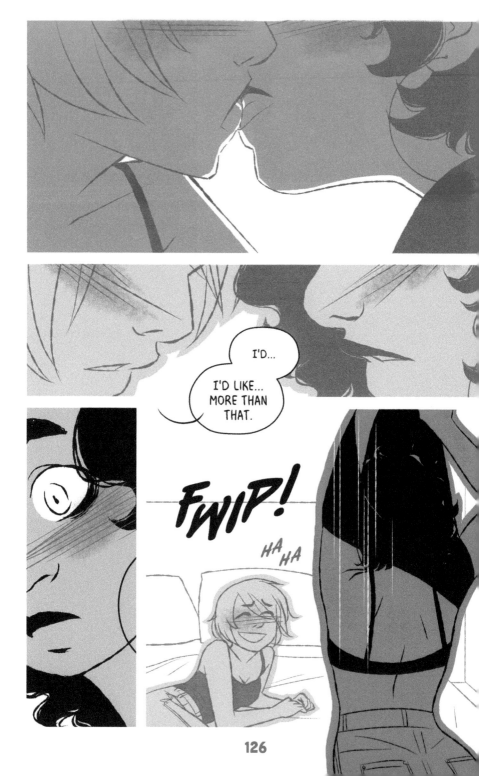

AH...
PRIYA...

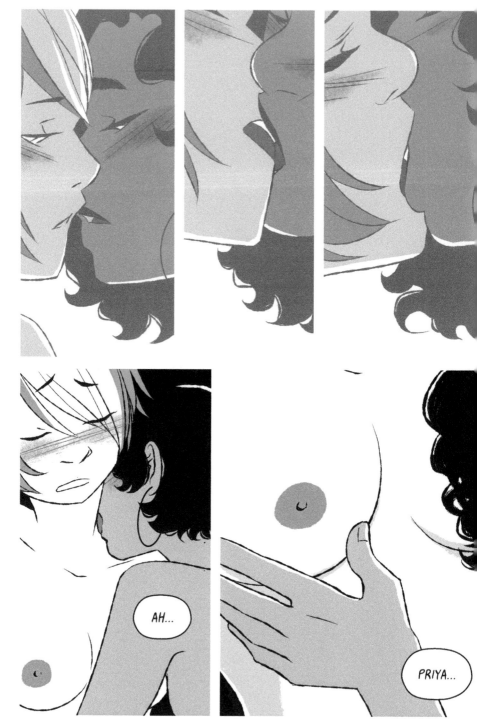

PRIYA...

SH*PF*

MM...

HAH...

AH...

AHHH
PRIYA—
AH...
AH...

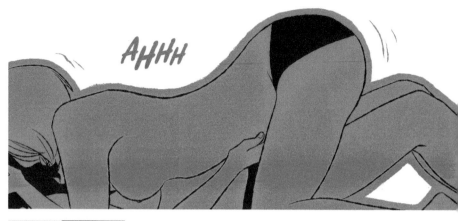

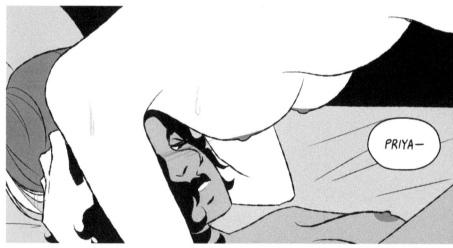

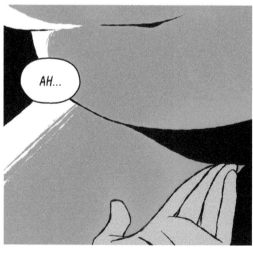

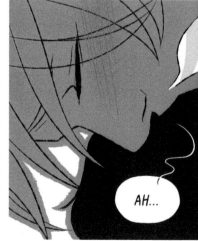

NN...
AH...
HEY...
EMI... CAN I...
M—
ME TOO...
I WANT... I... CAN I—

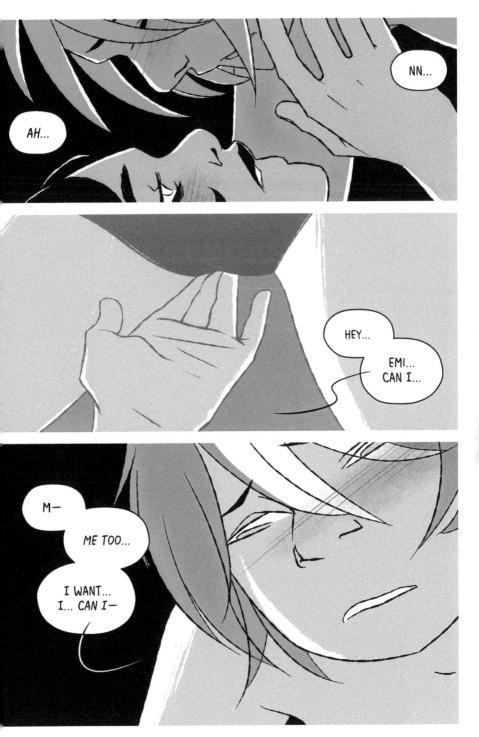

YES. GOD, EMI. GOD, I WANT YOU SO BAD.
I WISH I KNEW WHAT I WAS DOING.
JUST—
AH!
JUST...
JUST DON'T STOP...
AH—
SLIDE

PRIYA—
AH—
NN—
EMI—

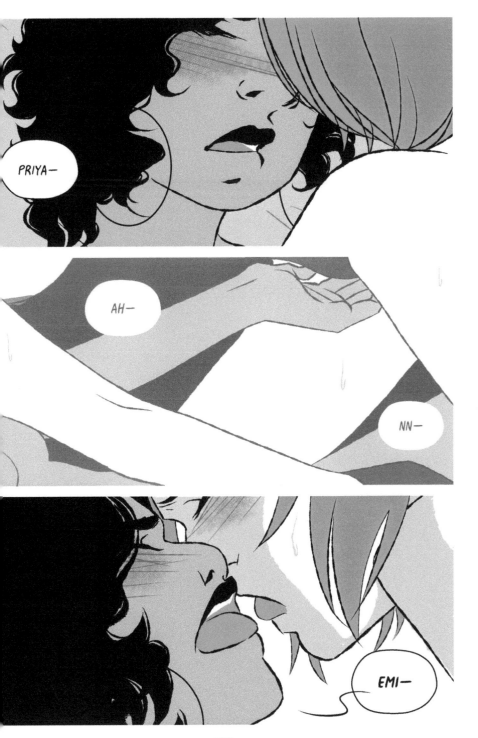

AH!
IS IT... ALWAYS LIKE THIS?
HAH...
HAH...
TOUCHING YOU...
MAKES ME DIZZY.
I DON'T WANT TO STOP.

AH!

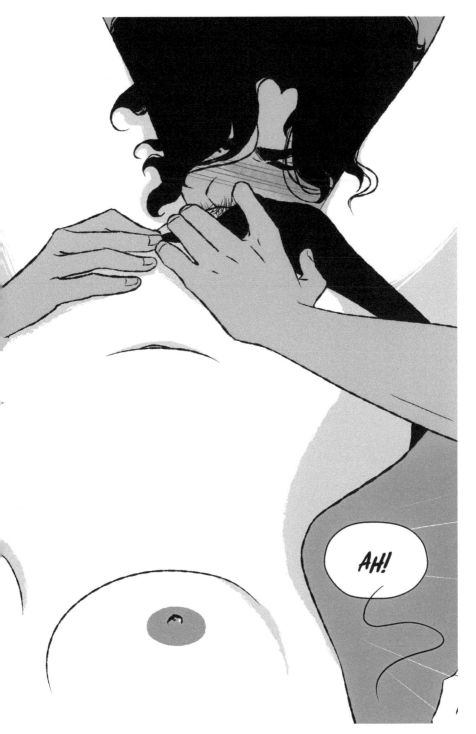

SO... DO WE CALL THEM "SEMPAI" NOW?
...
CALL... WHO?
YOU KNOW... ALEXIS... 'N HER GIRLFRIEND...
HA HA HA HA
OH GOD, DON'T YOU DARE...
GOD... THEY'LL TEASE US ENOUGH AS IT IS AFTER THIS... THEY'LL—
AH—

MY CAMERA!

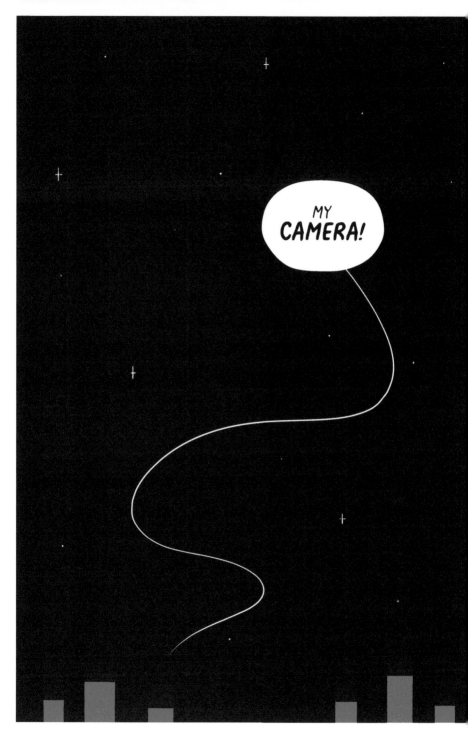

THE END

AUUGH, THEY'RE SO CUTE AND SINCERE AND I JUST WANT TO EAT THEM UP...
Grace
Alexis

HEY, SO... THERE'S THIS NEW BASEBALL SERIES...
TRUST ME, BABY. I KNOW.
Tommy
Sierra

HOW DID I LET YOU TALK ME INTO THIS...
Priya
Emi

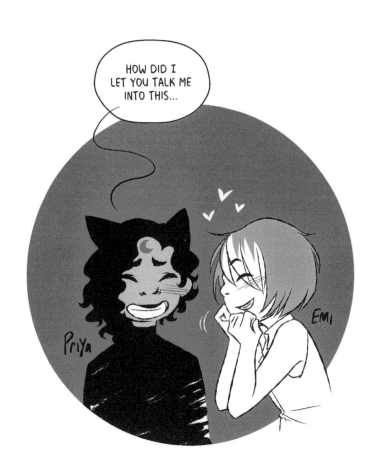

THANK YOOOOU!
Lee
Samirah

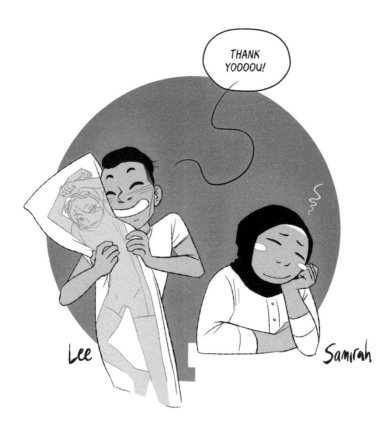

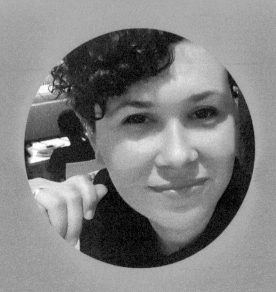

Niki Smith is a creator of fine comics (and some pretty trashy ones too). Since 2010, her erotic comics have been published through FilthyFigments.com, a collective of women and non-binary cartoonists dedicated to making naughty comics that everyone can see themselves in.

An American artist who now calls Germany home, Niki lives in Munich with her wife. Her work can be found at Niki-Smith.com.